W9-CLI-362

Copyright © 1996 by Nord-Süd Verlag AG, Gossau Zürich, Switzerland
First published in Switzerland under the title *Das ganz besondre Ostergeschenk*
English translation copyright © 1996 by North-South Books Inc.

First published in the United States, Great Britain, Canada,
Australia, and New Zealand in 1996 by North-South Books,
an imprint of Nord-Süd Verlag AG, Gossau Zürich, Switzerland.

Distributed in the United States by North-South Books Inc., New York.

Library of Congress Cataloging-in-Publication Data is available.
A CIP catalogue record for this book is available from The British Library.
ISBN 1-55858-573-7 (TRADE BINDING)
1 3 5 7 9 TB 10 8 6 4 2
ISBN 1-55858-574-5 (LIBRARY BINDING)
1 3 5 7 9 LB 10 8 6 4 2
Printed in Belgium

95052220

Dorothea Lachner

Smoky's Special Easter Present

Illustrated by Christa Unzner

Translated by Marianne Martens

North-South Books / New York / London

"Good morning, Smoky," Emma mumbled sleepily. "Are you ready for breakfast?"

"I've been ready for hours," thought Smoky. His stomach had been growling so loudly, he was surprised it hadn't woken Emma long before. He was getting hungry enough to gnaw on a chair leg or chew a slipper.

"Coming right up!" called Emma as she went to get him some food.

While Smoky ate, Emma drew a picture of the Easter Bunny. "You know, Smoky," she said, gazing at the picture, "this Easter I hope the Easter Bunny brings me something really special."

Smoky stopped eating. He loved Emma and wanted her to be happy. "I know!" he thought. "I'll go to the city to get her a special Easter present!"

Smoky hid behind a pair of boots until someone opened the front door. Then he sneaked out, leaping across the garden and through the gate.

He arrived at the bus stop just in time. Smoky watched the people boarding the bus. They each pressed something into the driver's hand and were allowed to get on the bus. Smoky thought quickly; then he plucked a flower from the hat of the woman in front of him and handed it to the driver. The driver laughed. "Aha!" he said. "You must be the Easter Bunny! Hop aboard!"

Smoky sat next to a woman who had a basket full of carrots on her lap. But he wasn't even tempted to nibble one because the motion of the bus was making him feel a bit sick.

Suddenly, two strong hands grabbed him. "Perfect!" a man shouted. "I've been looking for a special Easter present."

"So have I!" squeaked Smoky. He kicked and squirmed desperately until the man let go of him. Then Smoky jumped off the bus and hopped away.

Smoky had survived the swaying bus ride, the strong-armed man, and lots of traffic. He finally reached a huge shop. "Amazing!" he thought, peering in the window. "You just go in and take whatever you want. I've come to the right place." Excited, he entered the store.

A friendly saleslady asked if she could help him find something.

"I'm looking for an Easter present. I want something that's more special than all the Easter eggs in the world."

The saleslady wanted to know how much money Smoky could spend on the present.

Smoky shrugged. He didn't know for sure what money was, but he certainly knew that he didn't have any.

"If that's the case, I'm afraid we can't help you," said the saleslady, who was suddenly not as friendly as she had been.

Feeling sad, Smoky left the store. Dodging cars, motorcycles, and people, he made it safely to the river.

Sitting on the bank was a homeless man, who called to Smoky, "Why don't you come over here and relax a little?"

Smoky edged a little closer to the man and sat down next to him. He suddenly realized how tired he was. And hungry, too! If only he had finished his breakfast.

He nibbled on a clump of grass growing between some stones. It didn't even begin to fill him up.

"Looks like you haven't eaten in a while," said the homeless man, sharing a piece of bread with the bunny. "It must be frightening to be a rabbit, constantly running away from danger. Here, take my hat. Then you'll always have a place to hide." He plopped the hat on Smoky and went on his way.

It was a nice hat, but Smoky wasn't sure it was the right present for Emma. Suddenly Smoky heard a loud shriek behind him.

A girl with wild hair was waving at him. "Please wait," she called. "I just love your hat! Won't you swap it for my stuffed rabbit? He's called Mr. Ladislaus, and he's very special!"

Smoky was delighted. Mr. Ladislaus was just what he needed for Emma. Lugging the stuffed rabbit along with him, Smoky started for home. But he didn't get far.

All the dogs in the park had smelled him and were heading his way, growling and barking. Smoky knew he would only be able to save himself. Mr. Ladislaus was on his own. He ran for his life, out of the park and straight into more danger.

Barely avoiding being hit, Smoky found himself completely surrounded by honking cars and shouting people. The little bunny was terrified. Suddenly someone grabbed him by the scruff of his neck.

"There you are, you little escape artist!" a familiar voice scolded gently. It was Emma's father. He put Smoky in a big box.

Smoky sighed with relief. Then he curled up and went to sleep.

He was so exhausted, he didn't wake up until the next morning. He poked his nose out of the box and saw that he was back home, safe and sound. But it was Easter and Smoky didn't have the special present for Emma. He felt so bad about it that he tried to hide. But Emma found him.

"Oh, Smoky," she said, hugging and patting him. "Having you back is the best Easter present of all!"